Elizabeth

The Real
MOTHER GOOSE

Written and Illustrated by Ruth Doty

ELIZABETH, THE REAL MOTHER GOOSE

Library of Congress Catalog Card Number: 97-93225

ISBN 0-9658089-1-2

Edited by Carolyn Stollman

First Edition

Printed in the United States of America

To my grandchildren,

Alexandra, Elizabeth, Samantha and Ryan

To my husband,

for his patience and support

To my daughter, Susan,

for her encouragement and love

In the early part of the 1930s, long before children rode school buses, and long before homes had refrigerators, television or indoor bathrooms, there lived a young girl named Elizabeth. She lived on this wheat farm not far from Autwine, Oklahoma. This is her story as she lived it, wrote about it, and drew pictures of things close to her heart.

Harvest was a neighboring time on wheat farms in Oklahoma. The Knapp brothers owned a steam engine and threshing machine. My Papa had a team of mules and a hayrack which joined with ten others from our neighborhood. The harvest parade stretched a half a mile as it moved from one farm to the next to thresh the grain.

The farmer's wife prepared dinner for about 26 hungry men every day at noon until the threshing of the grain was finished on their farm. The harvesters finished at our place yesterday and now it was time for plowing.

Papa had left for town to have the plowshears sharpened. It was a very hot day and on his way out the door he turned to me and said, "It's so hot you can fry an egg on the roof of the barn. Lizzie, be sure and wear your shoes today or you'll blister your feet."

I was sprawled on the army cot on the front porch, daydreaming and spying ships and animals outlined in the fluffy white clouds sailing by.

Two long and two short rings interrupted my sky watching. Through the open window, I heard my Mama's voice say, "Yes, I can spare one of the girls. I know it is hard with a new baby."

When Mama hung up, she came out on the porch. "Elizabeth, Mrs. Knapp could use some help with baby Evelyn. The harvesters are at their farm today."

"I'd love to go to Mrs. Knapp's, Mama. I'll wear my yellow pinafore and shoes and walk through the wheat field."

Making my way across the pasture and entering the wheat field I felt the wheat stubble tickle my legs. Then a cottontail jumped up in front of me. Chasing rabbits was one of my favorite pastimes. I chased the rabbit down the rows of stubble until it disappeared into a gully. Breathing heavily, with sweat trickling down my back, I remembered my task and hurried on to Mrs. Knapp's.

Halfway there I crawled under the barbed wire fence dividing the two farms. There were no trees, no shade, no wind, no water, just the hot sun. My straw hat shaded my face and my mouth felt like cotton. I watched a hawk glide in the sky looking for its dinner.

Men with pitchforks were loading hayracks in the field. Billy, the water boy, was heading in their direction on his pinto pony. The threshing machine was belching out straw and making a new strawpile. I thought, what fun it would be to somersault down a new strawstack.

Mrs. Knapp had a glass of lemonade for me, and she said, "Elizabeth, your face is as red as a beet. Sit here and drink your lemonade while I nurse Evelyn."

When she finished nursing Evelyn, she handed her to me to rock.

"When she begins to get sleepy, put her in the cradle and rock it gently. Grandpa Knapp made the cradle special for Evelyn."

Evelyn was the first baby I had ever rocked. For a little while, her baby blue eyes were wide open and she never took them off of me. Smiling, I began talking to her in my softest voice, "You are a very pretty baby and you love to be rocked." Evelyn smiled and cooed contentedly. Softly I hummed Rockabye Baby, and soon she began to yawn, and it wasn't long before she drifted off to sleep.

Carefully I placed Evelyn in her cradle and rocked it gently. I was pleased my first venture with the new baby went so smoothly.

I went into the kitchen where Mrs. Knapp was cutting up chickens. She was pleased to know Evelyn had been so cooperative. "You must have experience with a baby," she said.

"Beginners luck. Evelyn is the first baby I ever rocked."

"On the table is a list of things you can do to help with dinner. It looks like we will have 26 hungry mouths to feed."

```
1. Set up washstand under the cottonwood
2. Pick strawberries
3. Set table for 13
4. Shuck corn
5. Snap greenbeans
6. Mix ice tea in the large pickle jar
7. Wash dishes after the first setting so we
   will have enough for the second setting
8. Help with cleanup
```

I went outside with towels, homemade tar soap, water pails, and wash pan. A couple of buckets of water from the windmill would get the harvest crew started on their cleanup.

Mrs. Knapp's geese were dozing in the shade of the cottonwood. The big gander in command had one eye open and tried to scare me off with his hissing, but I wouldn't give ground.

Mr. Knapp had a wonderful irrigated bed with huge strawberries in his fenced front yard. The bushes were loaded and I picked several gallon cans full.

By noon, the table was ready with fried chicken, mashed potatoes and gravy, corn on the cob, green beans, fruit salad with fresh strawberries, home-made buns and gallons of ice tea. The aroma of Mrs. Knapp's apple pies filled the air.

The first 13 hungry men filled the round table and ate and drank and drank and drank the ice tea.

When they finished, I hurried and cleared the table and washed the silverware and plates for the second serving. Mrs. Knapp did all the refills on the food for the second crew of 13 men.

When all the men were finished and we were doing the last of the dishes, Mrs. Knapp said, "I've a surprise for you, and some berries for your family, so I'll drive you home because you'll have too much to carry."

She put a basket covered with a towel on the table. "This is your surprise for being so much help with the meal and Evelyn. This is my way of saying thank you."

"Thank you, Mrs. Knapp, I loved rocking Evelyn and it was great fun picking the strawberries." Then I peeked under the towel covering the basket. What a surprise!

"Three goose eggs," I exclaimed. "Mrs. Knapp, I've always loved your geese. This is a wonderful gift."

"Read the instructions carefully, Elizabeth. It gives you all the directions about how to care for the eggs."

Instruction Sheet For Goose Eggs.
1. Mark your calendar for 30 days.
2. Place the eggs under a setting hen.
3. Three days before hatching, take a washpan full
   of warm water and test each egg. If they wiggle
   they will hatch. It makes the hatching easier.
4. Place a large coop in your fenced back yard.
5. Keep a pan of fresh water by their coop.
6. Fill a foot tub full of water so each can swim at birth.
7. Feed the goslings mash, cracked corn, cottage cheese,
   milk, grain, and fresh alfalfa.
8. If you have a pond, take them swimming, daily.
   GOOD LUCK!

Mrs. Knapp

July 1934

S	M	T	W	T	F	S
						①
2	3	4	5	6	7	8
9	10	11	12	13	14	15
16	17	18	19	20	21	22
23	24	25	26	27	28	29
㉚	31					

Papa didn't want me to set the eggs because he said geese are too messy, but Mama had raised ducks as a girl so she persuaded him to let me set the eggs.

I marked my calendar and Mama gave me Clarabelle, her largest Rhode Island red hen, to set on the three eggs. It was a nest full but this setting hen didn't seem uncomfortable.

Mama gave strict orders not to go near the setting house. All a setting hen needs is a large quantity of food and water about once a week. They are fussy and don't want to be disturbed.

According to Mrs. Knapp's instructions, three days before the eggs were to hatch, I took a pan of warm water and tested each egg. To my surprise, all three eggs made waves in the water. The soaking would make the hatching easier.

The first egg to hatch turned out to be the largest gosling. I was so excited I ran to the barn to show Papa my first baby. "Look, Papa, isn't my gosling a beauty?"

Papa looked up from his milking just in time to see the fuzzy little gander mess right down the front of my blouse, and he couldn't help but laugh. "I told you geese are a messy bunch."

I detoured by way of the windmill to rinse off the front of my blouse. It did make a terrible smell, but that is the trademark of all babies.

Papa and my brother, Elliot, built a large coop for the geese and put it in the fenced backyard along with the foot tub of water. I placed my first gosling carefully in the water and, would you believe it, he knew how to swim. Papa says they have a born instinct. As its head went under the tail came up, and this gosling loved the water from the start.

"You are a good swimmer," I whispered.

The next little gosling was born just after lunch, and Clarabelle was getting more frustrated by the hour. She didn't understand why the babies were so large and there was no peep, peep, peep that baby chicks make.

I named the second little gosling right away.

"Gandy, I like your funny little stomp dance."

The next morning Clarabelle was off her nest and waiting to make her escape the minute the door opened. The smallest gosling, alone in the nest, had a raw spot on its head where Clarabelle had pecked it. A perfectly beautiful petite little gosling looked up at me and I found myself saying, "Pansy, you will be a lovely goose some day."

I was grateful to Clarabelle that she decided to see the hatching to completion. But I can understand that being a mother to three goslings was a task she couldn't endure.

Once the geese were together, it didn't take long to see the big gander was a born leader, so I called him Andy, after Andrew Jackson.

I called Mrs. Knapp and told her, "All the eggs have hatched and the goslings are all white. Papa told me there are two ganders and one beautiful goose. Clarabelle will not accept the geese, so I am their mother."

Mrs. Knapp was glad to hear from me. "It is a miracle all the geese are white. We probably have 25 or 30 geese, but only seven white ones. Setting hens aren't good about accepting goslings once they are hatched. It is a blessing Clarabelle stayed long enough for all of them to hatch. You will be a good mother for the geese. Don't spoil them too much." Then she added "Evelyn is growing like a weed. She laughs a lot now. We will stop by one day to see the geese."

"Mrs. Knapp, I almost forgot to tell you I named the geese Andy, Gandy, and Pansy."

Mrs. Knapp commented, "Those are good names and thanks for calling."

I began the job of training my geese. Once a week, in my little black book, I neatly recorded how much they weighed, what they ate, amount of time they spent in the water, what kind of exercise they had daily, and anything outstanding that happened.

My ninth birthday was the last of August and I had spent nearly every waking moment with my geese. My birthday surprise was the three boxes Elliot and Papa made for the geese and the bonnet my sister, Mary Beth, made for Pansy. Papa and Elliot cracked the ice to make homemade ice cream. Mama baked a beautiful white coconut cake with Happy Birthday and nine candles on it. We all had a feast.

In the weeks following my birthday, my good-sized willow stick worked fine for instructing the geese. They learned my tapping signals and knew when to hop on their boxes. With much practice, the geese seemed to comprehend one, two, three, four, and five.

The geese learned early to like alfalfa which added protein to their diet. Pansy always chose sweet milk, Gandy feasted on cottage cheese, while Andy was fond of the mash and whole grain mixture.

Each day we walked to the alfalfa field. On some days we went on the long walk to the pond at the end of the pasture. Andy would lead and we walked single file. When I wore my bonnet Pansy tolerated hers.

On one of our walks, I had to use my willow stick to chase off a hawk who thought Pansy looked like dinner.

Summer passed quickly and school was to start in a few days. I began to worry about the geese, knowing my days of supervising were nearly over.

School started and Mama said the geese seemed lost for a few days, but after the first week, Andy stepped up and took command. They continued their daily walk to the alfalfa field. Andy and Gandy learned they could scare almost anything with their loud hissing.

It gave me a good feeling to see the geese become more independent. The geese knew I would be home around 4 pm and they lay dusting their feathers in the driveway.

When I got almost to the geese I sat on the ground and crossed my legs. Pansy came running and jumped into my lap. Gandy circled around me doing his famous stomp dance.

Andy was waiting for me to pick him up and toss him in the air so he could show me how far he could glide. As soon as he landed I always clapped my hands in approval. It was a joyful reunion time each day with the geese. It was also time for the surprise I had brought them in my lunch pail.

Gandy loved a piece of apple. Pansy had a sweet tooth and usually got half a cookie. Andy consumed what was left of my sandwich as he liked bread.

Andy took the lead coming up the driveway to the house. I took my lunch pail to the kitchen and quickly changed my clothes. I felt good about how everything was going. The geese were growing by leaps and bounds and they were developing in their ability to take care of themselves.

However, there was a problem. Andy was not comfortable about going to the pond at the end of the pasture. He had not been able to forget the day the hawk came so close to Pansy. The old hawk was constantly eyeing the geese. Andy and Gandy were fighters so whenever I was not along, they put Pansy in the middle instead of at the back. That had worked for now. They would fight to the end to protect Pansy. Instead of endangering their lives, Andy elected to take their daily swim in the horse tank. NOT A GOOD SOLUTION as far as Papa was concerned. The cows didn't appreciate it either.

It had been a hot August and September, and Andy, Gandy, and Pansy found that cement cools rapidly once the sun goes down. When the lights went off in the house, Andy marched his troop to the back porch. NOT A GOOD SOLUTION as far as Papa was concerned. "Messy," was Papa's description of the geese.

Caruso, our barnyard rooster, was more regular than any alarm clock. Precisely at 5 am every morning, he crowed his loudest. Papa's feet hit the floor and in no time he grabbed two milk buckets and headed for the barn.

The geese had not vacated the back porch at this early hour. Every morning Papa opened the screen door and began slip sliding in the terrible mess made by the geese.

Andy defended his territory with his loudest hissing, and Papa held his ground by swinging the buckets at Andy. The big gander would hiss even louder. This daily routine aggravated Papa immensely.

Not only was Andy hissing at Papa on the porch, but also at Papa when he was at the horse tank.

"Who does he think is the boss around here?" Papa muttered. "These geese have got to go."

Realizing there was a problem, early every morning I hurried and scrubbed the back porch before Papa came back with the milk. At night, the geese passed by my window going on maneuvers to the cool cement. Half asleep, I took my training stick and shooed them back to their coop. By morning they were back on the porch.

I scolded Andy and said, "You're going to end up on someone's Thanksgiving table."

It was late October and now the nights were cooler and the parade to the back porch stopped, but the daily swims in the horse tank did not.

One afternoon in early November, when I arrived home from school my geese were not waiting. There was a sick feeling in my stomach. Had the hawk feasted on Pansy? My search took me everywhere we had ever been, but still I couldn't find the geese. Finally, I went into the house and put my lunch pail on the cabinet. Papa and Mama were in the living room.

I asked, "Have you seen my geese?"

Papa said quickly, "I took the geese to the Community Sale and here's the money."

It came as a complete shock. "I don't want the money and I never want to know how much you sold them for. You could at least have let me return them to Mrs. Knapp." Crying uncontrollably, I stumbled to my room, changed my clothes, and went to the backyard. I sat down by the coop and couldn't stop crying. Sure, there was a problem but I never thought Papa would sell the geese without telling me first.

Three days passed, I had eaten very little and still was in a daze at school. The teacher asked my sister and brother what was wrong with me.

Mary Beth said, "Papa sold her geese."

Every night I prayed, "Dear God, please watch over my geese and don't let them end up on someone's Thanksgiving table." Choking up with tears overflowing, I cried myself to sleep.

On the fourth day, a letter arrived addressed to my father:
    Mr. Bill Gillespie
    Rural Route One
    Autwine, Oklahoma

The letter was from an old friend, John Weinbrenner.

Dear Bill,
You must have been in a hurry at the Community Sale. I bought your geese and you left before I could thank you.
You know the huge pond we used to swim and skate on as boys, well I keep geese there now. Your three geese love the water and the strawpile.
They are so healthy and put my geese to shame. What did you feed them?
If you have the time on Saturday I would be grateful if you dropped by and gave me more information about these beautiful geese.
Your old friend,
John Weinbrenner

While changing my clothes, Mama brought the letter and read it to me. I hugged her neck and burst into tears. It was such good news to know my three geese were safe.

That night I prayed, "Thank you, God, for watching over my geese."

I eagerly agreed to go visit Andy, Gandy and Pansy. I took leftover mash, grain, and cracked corn for Andy, sweet milk for Pansy, and some fresh cottage cheese for Gandy. Saturday, the time had finally arrived to go see Andy, Gandy and Pansy. I asked Papa to put in the truck the three boxes and the three feeding bowls that belonged to the geese. As an afterthought, I took along my willow training stick.

We arrived at the pond a little past 10 am. The geese were all on the water taking a swim. It was a beautiful pond and a perfect place for Andy, Gandy and Pansy. A strawpile nearby would keep them warm in the winter.

Papa introduced me to Mr. Weinbrenner and said, "Elizabeth is the one that raised the geese."

"Elizabeth, you sure did a fine job," Mr. Weinbrenner said.

"Mr. Weinbrenner, I brought some food and some fresh cottage cheese and sweet milk for the geese. Can we take these things down to the pond? I'm sure the geese will know me."

Mr. Weinbrenner smiled and said, "Let's go right on down to the pond."

I placed the boxes on the grass and filled the bowls as usual, then I sat down on the grass and crossed my legs.

Andy was always the observant one, and it didn't take a minute for him to recognize me. The three geese came swimming across the pond toward me. As they waddled through the grass, Pansy climbed right into my lap. Gandy did his dance around me and Andy was close enough I could hug his neck.

Mr. Weinbrenner was touched by what he saw.

The geese gobbled down the food, and when they finished I asked,

"Would you like to see how smart they are?"

"Yes, indeed," Mr. Weinbrenner said.

I picked up my willow stick and tapped it one time. Pansy flew to her box and took her place. Two taps! Gandy hopped on his box and did his stomp dance. Three taps! Andy circled around showing how he had mastered the goose step, then he jumped on his box.

Mr. Weinbrenner clapped.

I unwound my string and I held one end and Mr. Weinbrenner held the other. Five cards were hooked to the line. The cards had dots numbering one through five. I tapped five times and touched Andy's box with my stick. Quick as lightening he removed the card with five dots on it. Two taps and Pansy fetched the card with two dots. Four taps and Gandy had no problem bringing me the card with four dots. I demonstrated Drop the Handkerchief and Hide and Seek, too.

I asked Mr. Weinbrenner, "Is there an alfalfa field nearby? All geese should have that kind of protein in their diet."

"Just on the other side of the strawpile is a small field of alfalfa," Mr. Weinbrenner said. "I'm not sure if Andy found it or not."

"Can I please take them there?"

"My dear, I would be delighted for you to take them. Your dad and I need to catch up on our visiting." I went off with the geese to the alfalfa field.

Mr. Weinbrenner turned toward my father and said, "We don't live five miles apart and we never seem to get together like our parents did. I'm sure you remember this pond where we spent many hours swimming and sailing on that old raft."

Papa chuckled, "Those were the good old days."

"Tell me, why did you get rid of the geese?"

Papa answered, "Times have been hard and it's our egg and cream money that buy the groceries. The geese didn't have a pond to swim in so they spent a great deal of time in the horse tank. The cattle refused to drink the water so our cream production was down. Also, the geese chose the cement back porch as a place to sleep at night rather than their coop. I had to face that mess every morning. Elizabeth knew she had a problem. The geese are smart and it broke her heart when I sold them. Your letter was an answer to her prayers and I'm grateful, too."

"Elizabeth is welcome anytime to come and visit the geese. I had no idea they were so intelligent. I'm on the County Fair Board and we've been looking for some unusual performance for Saturday when the kids are out of school. Could Elizabeth exhibit the geese and put on a show?"

"I would leave that decision up to Elizabeth."

I returned from the alfalfa field and Mr. Weinbrenner asked, "Elizabeth, would you consider exhibiting the geese at the fair and doing a Saturday performance with Andy, Gandy and Pansy?" Before I could answer he added, "I'm on the County Fair Board and I believe they would pay you $10.00 for the performance. Think about it and I will get back to you on Monday."

The County Fair Board was delighted to have the geese and me for a Saturday, 10 am performance. Mr. Weinbrenner called on Monday and it didn't take me long to say, "I will be happy to show the geese and do a program."

"I have some good wooden crates and I will take the geese to the Fair, but you will need to furnish all the food and take care of the geese. We can leave about 8 am on Thursday if you can miss school on Thursday and Friday?" Mr. Weinbrenner said.

"Mr. Weinbrenner, please put the boxes with their names on them, and also their feeding bowls in the truck. I'll do the rest. Thank you so much. If you will hold on the line for a minute, I'll check with Mama and Papa about missing school."

Mr. Weinbrenner was pleased when I returned and said, "I'll be ready at 8 am on Thursday."

I was pretty excited about the performance. I spent many hours at the Weinbrenner pond reviewing with the geese everything they knew.

It was hard for me to realize they were no longer babies but fully grown geese. Mama said, "It's time to cut your apron strings."

I knew my love for Andy, Gandy and Pansy would always be in my heart and nothing would ever change that.

The next morning my mother showed me the newspaper, the headline read:

ELIZABETH, The Real Mother Goose
To Perform Saturday at Fairgrounds

Judging of the geese was on Friday. There were no other geese that measured up to Andy, Gandy and Pansy. I stayed close by to give support to the geese. Being penned up had made Andy a bit grumpy.

One Judge asked, "Did you raise the geese and if so, what did you feed them?"

I supplied the details and reached in the pen and patted Andy's back. I didn't want him hissing at the Judge.

"No question, definitely Grand Champions and Best of Class," the other Judge commented. Then they attached the large purple ribbon on their pen.

At the end of the performance, I bent down and put on Pansy's bonnet and tied ribbons on Andy and Gandy, then they took their bows. Everyone stood and cheered as we left the stage.

The performance was a huge success and the County Fair Board paid a $5.00 bonus plus the $10.00 promised because so many people said it was the best show they had ever seen.

The PTA (Parent-Teacher Association) at Center School, District 67, had a large picture made at the fair of me with Andy, Gandy and Pansy. It was quite a surprise when I returned to school and saw the picture hanging between Washington and Lincoln at the front of the classroom. On the blackboard, there was a big sign students had made that said, "ELIZABETH, THE REAL MOTHER GOOSE."

Each Saturday I continued to take treats to Andy, Gandy and Pansy at the Weinbrenner pond. In late spring, Pansy surprised me with three baby goslings. Elliot teased me saying, "Elizabeth, that makes you a Grandmother!"